If Chicken Tasted Like Chocolate

a picky eater story

Written by Charles Gennaro
Illustrated by Shannon Howell

Edited by Cindy L. Freeman

ISBN: 978-1-945990-41-0

High Tide Publications, Inc.
Deltaville, Virginia 23043

www.HighTidePublications.com

Printed in the United States of America

First Edition

Dedicated to picky eaters
and the parents
who try to feed them

Hi.

I'm Jack and
this is my story.

I used to be a
picky eater.

Well, I guess it's best to start at the beginning.

As far back as
I can remember,
eating new foods was
always hard for me.

First, it was the oatmeal...

Even the airplane spoons and silly faces would not make me eat that food.

I will tell you...
There was one thing
I DID love to eat.
The one thing
I could eat
day and night.
The most amazing,
wonderful,
incredible thing
I have ever tasted.

chocolate!

My love for chocolate began long ago...
I've loved chocolate ever since I went to Hershey, Pennsylvania and tasted chocolate for the first time.

There was a moment when it seemed that my father finally figured it out.

He was holding a box of chocolate.

I grabbed the piece from his hand and shoved it into my mouth.

It was a prune!

But then my troubles began all over again.

Short noodles,
long noodles,
white rice,
brown rice,
grilled cheese...yes, they put cheese on bread and cooked it.

My little brother seemed to be doing just fine.

Whatever you put on his plate...

HE ATE!

Lunch time at school was a little tricky.

An apple, a banana, and a sandwich. Who would want that?

I didn't care if I had to starve!

None of it for me!

When we would go to the city, my dad always stopped to get a hotdog.

Thankfully, when I went to Grandma and Grandpa's house, I never had to worry.

They always served my favorites...anything made from chocolate.

My dad would try to bribe me with a toy if I would have a bite of something new.

But all the toys in the world
would never get me to eat

oatmeal

or

grilled cheese

or

spaghetti

or that

SHRIMP

Dad was holding in his hand!

That night, I wandered into the kitchen. "What are you cooking, Dad?" I asked.

He opened the oven door, bent over and pulled out a cooked

Chicken!

My worst nightmare!

"I can't do it, Dad. I can't do it, I tell ya! I just can't!"

My dad looked so sad. "I am beginning to have my doubts that we will ever find a new food you like," he said. "You cannot live on just chocolate."

One night, we all sat down for dinner. My dad and my little brother ate their chicken, peas, and sweet potatoes.

I just stared at my plate.

Finally, my dad looked at me sitting there, refusing to eat anything.

"Son, I have an idea. What if we could make chicken taste like chocolate? Would you eat it then?"

"I would try, for sure!" I said.

"I think I see a twinkle in your eye...what are you thinking son?"

"Dad, I'm thinking about what you just said...

could chicken taste like chocolate!"

I closed my eyes. Carrots!

I imagined a carrot dripping with chocolate!

"Dad, what if carrots, cabbage

or celery tasted like chocolate clumps?"

"Or cucumbers,
cantaloupe
or
corn

crunched like
chocolate chunks?"

"And cherries,
clams,
or cottage cheese
chewed like
chocolate lumps?"

"All this time I imagined these foods tasted terrible. So...yes, Dad! I can imagine all these things tasting like chocolate. "

My dad just stared at me. "Are you sure son? Afer all this time..."

"There is only one way to find out," I said.

"Let's give it a try!"

I ate a noodle...
it tasted like chocolate.
Then rice...
it tasted like chocolate.
And yes...oh yes.
Even the chicken
tasted like chocolate.

I didn't know why my food
began to taste like chocolate,
and I really didn't care.

After that night,
life was much easier
and a whole
lot sweeter.

Moral of the story...I wasn't afraid of what different foods were going to taste like. To me, everything tasted like chocolate.

I am older now and have a family of my own. I eat all kinds of different foods.

But chocolate will always be my favorite.

About the Illustrator

Shannon Howell (nee Gebhardt) is a laboratory assistant, student, and illustrator.

She was born on Long Island, New York and grew up on Long Island and in Oklahoma.

She spent much of her childhood in creative outlets and dreamed of one day growing up to become an artist.

In addition to her artwork, she found her calling for social services during early adulthood and is studying for her degree in the social work field.

Shannon was honored to assist Charles in turning his inspiration *If Chicken Tasted Like Chocolate* into a reality.

This is her first illustration work.

Shannon and her husband Kip, and Labrador, Emma, live in Oklahoma.

About the Author

Charles Gennaro is a Physical Therapist and Author.

He grew up in the small town of Mastic Beach, New York and attended

William Floyd High School. He graduated from the State University of New York at Cortland in 1993.

The never-ending debate, negotiating, and yes…sometimes bribery, for his children to try new foods is an experience that many parents can relate to.

His book I*f Chicken Tasted Like Chocolate* exhibits a low stress approach to children's eating habits and believes life tends to be a whole lot sweeter through humor.

His sons served as inspiration for the creation of this story during a visit to Hershey, PA. He was fortunate enough to collaborate with illustrator Shannon Howell on this project.

Charles now lives in Manorville, New York.

Made in the USA
Middletown, DE
25 March 2020